Door Village School

SQUEEZE A SNEEZE

BILL MORRISON

Houghton Mifflin Company Boston

To David, Robb, and Julie

Library of Congress Cataloging in Publication Data

Morrison, Bill.
    Squeeze a sneeze.

    SUMMARY: Suggests putting words together into
funny rhymes such as "Bake a cake for your favorite
snake."
    1. Nonsense-verses. [1. Nonsense verses.
2. English language--Rime] I. Title.
PZ8.3.M825Sq   811'.5'4   76-62503
ISBN 0-395-25151-6

If you're sitting around
with nothing to do,
I've got a game
to play with you.
You take some words
and make them rhyme.
It's a wonderful way
to pass the time.

To start your own game, just look all around
and pick out some things that have the same sound.
Then mix them together and you'll surely find
the funniest pictures will dance in your mind.
You're using words, and words, as you know,
will help you out wherever you go.

Here are some words that I keep in my hat,
like pickle, and tickle, and poor alleycat.
I'll scrabble them up and pick out a few,
and make up some rhymes that are funny and new.

Can you tickle
a pickle
for a nickel?

Or sit on
a flea's knees

Cool your tea
with the wings of a bee

Share a pear
with a
hungry bear

Bake a cake
for your favorite snake

Buy a tall hat
for a poor alleycat

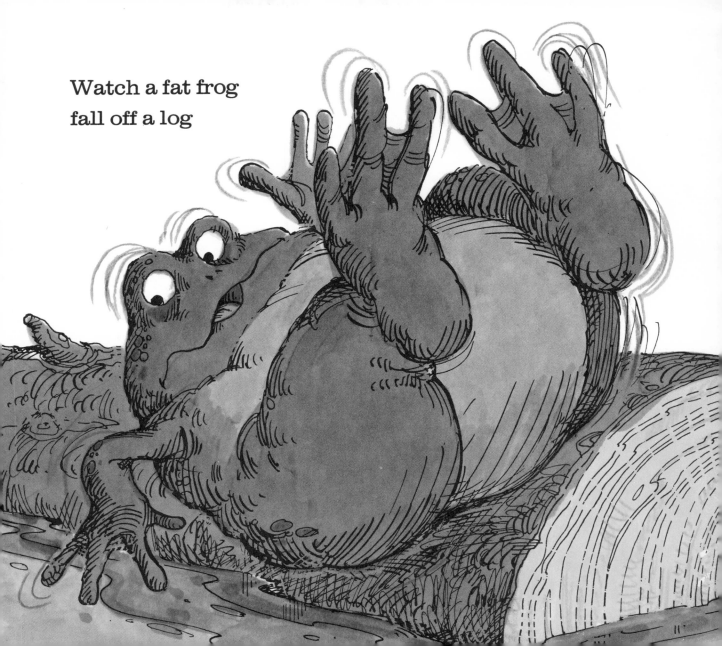

Watch a fat frog
fall off a log

Find a bug
on your rug
and give it a hug

Hit a fly
in the eye
with a blueberry pie

Make a man sneeze
with a mouth full of peas

Make sure it's dark
if you bark
at a shark

Paint a bean green
to give to a queen

Stuff a goose
and a moose
in a tiny caboose

Take a snail
for a sail
in a polka dot pail

Try your own words and have some fun.

I've got to go, I've got to run.

I've no more time to make a rhyme.

See you later, alligator!

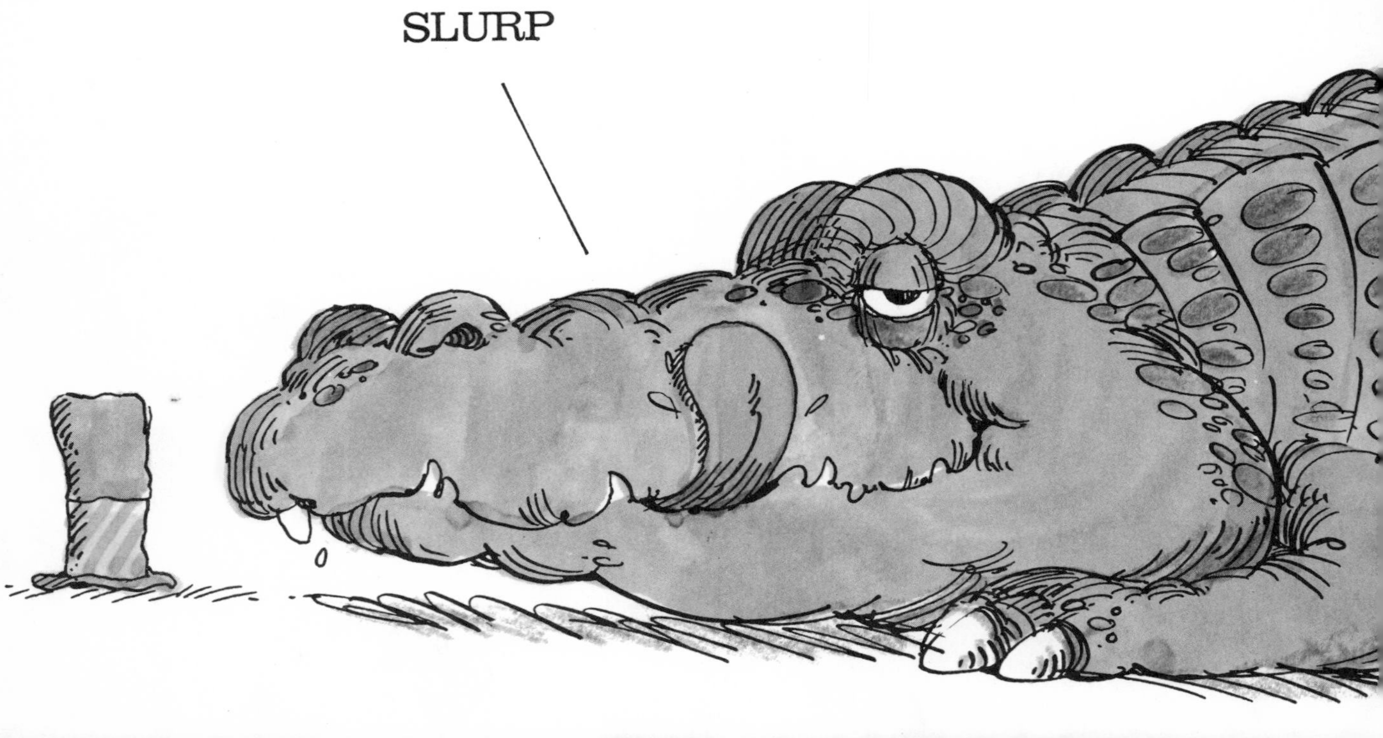
SLURP

BURP